THE TRIPLE MIRROR

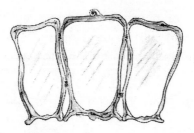

To Marianne,

With warmest love and

blessings,

Ema.

Plymouth 17.01.05

GreenSpirit

Greenspirit, the Association for Creation Spirituality in Britain, is part of a widespread movement exploring different ways of seeing, and living in, our world. More and more people are realising that we cannot continue using the earth and her creatures as if we owned them, increasing the gap between the haves and the have-nots in society, and despoiling the earth.

New insights from ecology, psychology and the physical sciences, linking the latest Western knowledge and understanding to traditional wisdom, can lead us to a different way of perceiving our presence on earth. We need a profound shift in thinking and feeling to convert the present over-consumption to a simpler, more compassionate way of living here.

For further information see: www.greenspirit.org.uk

THE TRIPLE MIRROR

by
Erna Chrispeels
&
Michael Colebrook

Illustrations
Meier Williams

Association for Creation
Spirituality

Published by GreenSpirit
The Association for Creation Spirituality,
1 Sea Trout Mews, Staverton,
Totnes, Devon TQ 9 6PA
Registered Charity No. 1045532
http://www.greenspirit.org.uk

ISBN 0 9532551 6 6

Distributed by GreenSpirit Books
14 Beckford Close, Warminster
Wilts BA12 9LW
www.greenspirit.org.uk/books

Printed By PlaneTree Printing Ltd.,
Llanidloes, Powys

To Oscar, Rachel and Brydie,
our grandchildren

ACKNOWLEDGEMENTS

We would like to thank Rev Freddie Denman who read an early draft to the children of Sparkwell Primary School and told us how they responded.
Also we thank Jake Daykin, a neighbour and school-teacher for helpful comments.
Lastly we thank our friend Christine Avery who made an excellent job of copy editing the text and encouraging us throughout the birth of this book.

CONTENTS

1

Surprised by an Earthquake

$\mathcal{I}$t was Mum's idea to book a cottage overlooking Loch Ness. She's studying geology at the University and wanted to have a closer look at the Great Glen. It was Dad's idea to travel to Inverness by train, leaving the car at home in York.

"It'll be better for the planet," he said, "and more fun than being cooped up in a car."

And it was Brydie's and my idea to go monster hunting. I am Bran and I am eleven years old. Brydie is my sister, she is ten. Brydie has a large pet brown rabbit called Amber. She likes to sing when she is carrying her about. There is an old willow tree at the bottom of our garden which she loves to climb. I prefer books. Dad owns a bookshop near the Cathedral called 'Body and Soul' and I go with him whenever I can to give him a hand.

The autumn half term arrived at last. We packed plenty of games and books in our rucksacks. Gran gave us some pocket money to spend in the buffet car on the long trek to Scotland. We were all really glad when the train pulled into the station at

Inverness where a rented car was waiting for us. We followed the instructions Mrs McPherson had sent us and found our way to her cottage easily. It was called 'Newhaven'. What a name!

"Welcome to Scotland," she said as she opened the door. She was wearing a thick colourful cardigan and a tweedy sort of skirt. She proudly showed us round. The living room had a low ceiling and a creaky floor. There was a sweet smoky smell in the room coming from an open fire.

"Is that a peat fire, Mrs MacPherson?" I asked.

"It certainly is. I like the traditional ways. I am sure you'll get to like it too. There's a good stack of sods under the shelter at the back of the house, so help yourselves."

"How do we light it in the morning?" I asked, trying to sound practical.

"Och laddie," she said, "a peat fire never goes out."

While I mulled over this piece of ancient Scottish lore, Mum had started unpacking and Brydie laid claim to a small bedroom from which you could see a bit of Loch Ness. It had bunk beds, but that would do Brydie and me nicely for a week.

During our long train journey north there had been quite a bit of talk about the Loch Ness monster. Mum had explained that though the loch was now cut off from the sea, a long time ago dinosaurs could easily have swum into it. When Brydie asked Mrs MacPherson about this she had a twinkle in the eye when she said, "Lassie, you never know!"

2

"If you need me, I stay in the summer house at the bottom of the garden," I heard her say as she left us to get on with unpacking.

Before going to sleep we talked about what we might do the following day.

"I'm ready to go monster hunting," said Brydie.

"So am I. I'm sure there are lots of places near by where we can get a good view of the loch."

But, when we woke up it was raining. We spent the day getting organised and settling in. Brydie volunteered to keep the living room fire well supplied with peat. After lunch I started browsing through Mrs MacPherson's books.

"Look what I've found Brydie. A book called *The Encyclopaedia of the Loch Ness Monster.*"

We spent the rest of the afternoon happily going through it. There were pictures and stories and accounts of expeditions. Lots of useful information. It was amazing how many people had claimed to have seen the monster.

That night we went to bed more than ever determined to hunt for the monster. When we woke up, Brydie, who could look out through the window from her top bunk, said excitedly, "Bran, come and look, the loch looks fantastic. The sky's blue and the mountain tops are covered in snow."

After breakfast we sat on an old bench in front of the cottage. The autumn sun was warm on our faces. A black cat jumped onto Brydie's lap. Mrs MacPherson came up the path carrying a basket.

"Good morning," she said. "I see that you have made friends with Lucky. She is a bit of a scratcher, mind.

"I am out early to collect some apples while the weather lasts. It's Halloween tomorrow. I expect some Guisers will come knocking and I like to be ready.

"I hope you're not too old for some 'dooking', for I'm planning a wee party."

Then she added, looking wistfully at the distant hills, "It's the time when the veils between the present and the past are at their thinnest, when the living and the dead feel close to each other."

We weren't quite sure what she meant but the idea of a Scottish Halloween sounded fun – if a little mysterious – and we accepted the invitation gladly.

The coming day seemed full of possibilities. Our holiday was going to be OK after all. Brydie and I set off on our monster hunt with sandwiches and a drink and Dad's new binoculars.

"Be sure to bring them back!" he shouted.

We spent a good bit of the morning building a den for ourselves with branches and dry bracken from which we could see a good stretch of the loch. At last we had joined the many hunters who had come here in the hope of solving the mystery of the monster, the dinosaur of the deep. All our doubts about a Scottish holiday had melted away. Our cameras, a Christmas gift from Gran, would provide the photos needed for us to become famous.

Easier said than done. The only ripples on the loch were those made by speedboats or other small craft.

As we came in through the door of 'Newhaven' Dad asking Mum about her day.

"The Great Glen's a frightening place, Peter. It really is hard to interpret the geological map here."

Dad had spent the day in Inverness and had discovered an interesting little bookshop where he found a second hand copy of a book by a scientist called Charles Darwin. In 1831 he sailed from Plymouth in a ship called the *Beagle*. The voyage was an expedition of discovery to South America and Darwin's job was to look at the animals and plants there. When he came home to England he developed a theory about how new species of animals and plants appear on Earth.

"You see," said Dad, "he found that very simple life forms were transformed over millions of years into more complicated ones – not only their bodies but also their awareness. We call it evolution. It's a wonderful story – a sacred story. I have some excellent books and videos in the shop that you can look at when we get home. They tell you how the whole universe has evolved from the first fantastic burst of energy called the Big Bang."

"And what about your day?"

"Nessy kept to the deeps all day, but we're hoping for better things tomorrow," I said.

"Well, in science a negative result is also worth noting down." he said, reassuringly.

"On our way home, we met a man with a lot of photographic equipment," said Brydie. "He said that he had a very good picture at home – definitely more than ripples, a possible sighting. He told us to keep up the good work."

"We're definitely going back tomorrow," I added.

Dad had prepared the evening meal. It was spaghetti bolognese with a mixed salad and warm garlic bread, a family favourite. We were allowed a glass of wine as it was a special meal and there was to be a surprise for 'afters'. We were all in high spirits, eating large helpings of spaghetti.

Suddenly, everything on Mrs MacPherson's old-fashioned table started to rattle, the windows seemed to shudder and the roof tiles clattered. A pot of yellow chrysanthemums that Mrs MacPherson had put on the windowsill juddered towards the edge and fell off with a crash. Mum shouted, "It's an earthquake. Quick! Run outside!"

As I ran my feet felt unsteady on the cottage floor. Pictures of crumpled buildings and people being rescued from under tons of rubble flashed through my mind. Please not me! My heart thumped as I reached the driveway.

We all looked at one another. "That was really scary, Dad!" I said.

"Yes, very!" said Brydie. "Agreed," said Dad.

We were all safe and sound and the cottage was still standing. All the same, my legs were still shaking. The earthquake couldn't have lasted more than ten or twelve seconds but it seemed a lot longer. I gave Brydie a reassuring hug and so did Mum – it became hugs all round.

Nothing more happened and we were soon wondering whether it was safe to go back inside when we saw Mrs MacPherson walking briskly up the path. "Are you alright?" she asked.

"It was an small earthquake, Mrs MacPherson," said Mum.

"Yes I know, it's happened several times before now," she replied. "Folk round here call them tremors. You get used to them but this one was bigger than usual."

We were all a bit shaken to say the least. Mum asked Mrs MacPherson in for a cup of tea. She helped to clear up the mess of the broken pot.

"That doesn't happen often," she said calmly.

Dad fetched the surprise chocolate gateau he had bought in Inverness. It was like a little party with Mrs MacPherson giving us more useful tips about monster watching. We were all relaxing, especially Mum who gave us a bit of a lecture about earthquakes and the Great Glen. "Have a look at my map," she said.

"You see, it's like this," she went on. "Inverness is here on the east coast and Fort William here on the west coast. In between is the Great Glen with Loch Ness, Loch Oich and Loch Ochy. It's about 80 kilometres long. The Great Glen lies on what we geologists call a fault line, which is rather like an enormous crack in the land.

"Most of what is now Scotland was once part of a land mass called Laurentia. But, about 400 million years ago, the land masses that are now the rest of Britain and most of Europe collided with Laurentia – it was more like a slow sideways crunch, rather than a collision – and it lasted millions of years. The crunch caused several massive cracks to appear and the land in between was dragged sideways. The Great Glen is what remains of one of these cracks.

"Even today, 400 million years later, the rocks are still settling down. That's why there are small earthquakes here."

"Well, well, nobody ever told me that before," said Mrs MacPherson. "It's time for me to be off. I still have to make a batch of griddle cakes for tomorrow. Good night!"

That night Brydie and I had a lot of talking to do.

"I think Mrs MacPherson knows more than she lets on," said Brydie.

"I think so too," I replied. "What are griddle cakes?"

"I'm not sure," said Brydie, "but I think they are small pancakes."

We went on for some time about Dinosaurs, earthquakes, Mum and Laurentia, Dad and the evolution of life on earth – "You know Bran, I have a feeling that it all hangs together somehow."

When Dad shouted, "off to sleep now, you two, and I mean it," we knew that our talking time was up. Brydie switched off the light. What would tomorrow bring?

2

We Meet the Great Mother

We woke up early and decided on another monster watch. We felt there was a chance the earthquake might have disturbed Nessy and she might come to the surface to see what had happened.

We set off straight after breakfast with plenty of provisions for the whole day.

"I want you back by 5 o'clock," Mum warned. "Don't forget Mrs MacPherson's Halloween party."

What was it that she had said again – "the veils between the present and the past are at their thinnest at Halloween" – "What do you think she meant?" said Brydie as we walked briskly in the cool morning air.

We soon reached our den of yesterday but we decided to walk on and try to find a new spot, but as we walked a sudden thick mist came down around us. Dad had told us what to do if this happened. "Find some shelter and just sit tight and wait for it to clear. Whatever you do don't try to walk on," he had said.

So this is what we did. After a bit the mist seemed to get a lot clearer, at least in the direction in which we had been going before the mist came down. We decided to walk on. It was a decision that we would never forget because, suddenly, we weren't in the Great Glen any more! We found ourselves on a straight and narrow track somewhere in what looked as if it had once been a jungle but now all the trees were bare; the ground was covered with dead leaves and everything was grey and dreary.

"What's happening here?" asked Brydie.

"I think we may have found out what Mrs MacPherson was talking about," I replied. "I think we have just walked through a veil, but I don't know whether this is the past, the present, or the future."

The light was fading fast. All we could see on either side of the track were eyes, great big shiny eyes staring at us as if they were accusing us of killing their forest. Brydie took my hand as we hurried on.

"It's scary here," she said, "what are those weird noises?"

Then, on the path in front of us we could see a pair of green eyes and as we got nearer the form of a large grey wolf emerged from the gloom. It was sitting right in the centre of the path, as if it had been waiting for us. We stopped and stood as if rooted to the spot. The wolf got up and walked slowly towards us.

"I am Akka, a she-wolf and leader of my pack. We don't understand why, but some humans have destroyed the jungle that was our home. You can help us."

"How?" I managed to stammer.

"You must find the Triple Mirror. It will show you what you have to do."

"But where do we look for this mirror?" asked Brydie who seemed to be less scared of the wolf than I was. But without replying Akka just walked away and disappeared in the gloom.

We still stood there not knowing what to do or what to make of the wolf's message when Brydie said "Listen, I can hear something, it sounds like music."

We walked towards it at once. As we went along we realised that it wasn't gloomy any more and also it was getting very warm. Despite the heat we walked faster. The music got louder and louder and the light was brighter then ever. Fantastic flares and fireworks were shooting out in all directions. In some mysterious way we had been led to the biggest fireworks display we had ever seen or would ever see again. We were spellbound.

"Some kind of brilliant party is going on here, Brydie. I hope we can join in."

"But where are the people?" she said. "And where exactly are we?"

Suddenly we saw a tall, stately woman coming towards us. She seemed to appear from nowhere. She was dressed in a long multi-coloured coat and she carried a large bag over her shoulder.

"She is smiling at us," whispered Brydie. "It's almost as though we're expected."

"Welcome to the Very Beginning," she said in a kindly voice. "Don't be afraid, I am the Great Mother of the Universe. I have been given many names, but you may call me Great Mother for short. And you are Bran and Brydie from planet Earth, I believe."

"Yes, Great Mother," we answered politely, wondering how she knew our names.

"I'm sorry it has taken you so long to get here. It was a bit of a nightmare wasn't it?" We nodded. "I'm very glad that you've arrived at last," she said. "I believe the earthquake in the Great Glen last evening was quite a surprise?"

"Yes, Mum told us that it was caused by something that happened a very long time ago," I said.

"Would you like to go on an amazing adventure with me, and see more about the very beginnings of planet Earth? I call it the Great Journey of Wonders."

We were speechless. So much was happening so quickly. Could we refuse an invitation from the Great Mother of the Universe?

"What do you think Brydie?" I said, playing for time.

"I think it sounds exciting," she replied.

She turned towards the Great Mother. "Do you think we'll find the Triple Mirror that Akka the wolf told us about?"

"You may, if you let the mirror find you," said the Great Mother.

"Will we see Nessie?" I asked,

"This journey will take us nearly fourteen billion years, and on the way you will certainly meet some of her cousins."

"Fourteen billion years! But we don't live that long," I said. "Are you taking us time travelling Great Mother?"

"I believe I am," she replied with a smile.

"You'll need some travel gear," she added, handing each of us a shimmering, grey-blue, zip-up suit and a pair of handsome yellow boots. That's all you'll need. I like to travel light and so should my companions.

"These suits are like a second skin. They will protect you from the intense heat and will also keep you warm if it gets unbearably cold. Your boots are magic. With each step you take you will be travelling through time."

"Are you ready for this journey?"

I still hesitated. What if we got stuck somewhere, accidents are always happening. On the other hand it could be our way home. It was Brydie who decided.

"We certainly are!" she said, pulling on her new suit and yellow boots.

"A little more information before we set off," said the Great Mother. "Where we are starting from – that is, where we are now – is the Very Beginning of the Universe.

"All the energy contained in the Very Beginning and now bursting out all round us will be transformed into countless wonders over the best part of fourteen billion years. But more of that later on."

"Are we in the Big Bang?" I asked.

"Humans have given it many names and tried to describe it in many ways," she replied with a smile.

The Very Beginning was a terribly hot place, so we were glad to be off. The Great Mother took us by the hand, and suddenly we were moving. Where were we going? All I knew was that Brydie and I were trusting someone with whom we were going to share an extremely long, difficult and possibly dangerous journey.

3

Clouds of Hydrogen

" $\mathcal{T}$ ime travel is easy," said the Great Mother, "just walk in step with me for a while," as we took long strides in our yellow boots. It was a strange sensation. It's not so easy to walk when there is nothing to put your feet on and it was amazing to know that with every step we took thousands and thousands of years were passing, and yet we didn't grow a day older!

"I love my magic boots, Brydie, they fit really snugly."

"That makes a change, you usually make a fuss about new boots."

We strode with increasing confidence and soon began to look around us. It was getting much cooler and the light wasn't nearly as bright.

"This is a short haul, only about five hundred million years." said the Great Mother. "I believe I can see the spot we're heading for."

It was obvious that this time travel would take a lot of getting used to. When we arrived all we could see was a grey stone bench floating in space.

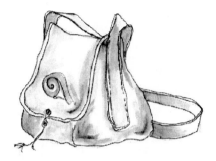

"This is all we need," the Great Mother said, sitting down and opening her bag.

"Come and join me. It was too hot at the Very Beginning for you to stay long so I packed some sandwiches. They're rather ordinary I'm afraid but I have lots of delicious old fashioned apple juice."

We had been too busy to think about food and drink but at the mention of it we suddenly felt hungry and very thirsty.

As we were eating, I asked a question. "Great Mother, where exactly in the universe was the Very Beginning? Was it right in the centre?"

"The universe doesn't have a centre, because it doesn't have an edge," she replied. "The only answer to your question is that the Very Beginning is everywhere."

"Everywhere? But things can't be everywhere."

"Are you everywhere too, Great Mother?" added Brydie, who seemed to understand the riddle.

"I certainly am," she said with a smile.

"You see Bran, at the Very Beginning the universe came into being. It contained everything that is and ever will be. But this everything – time, space, matter, energy and awareness – grows and changes and flows like a river, on and on. It evolves. I'll soon be showing you how this happens.

"As for you Brydie, people on Earth have puzzled over your kind of question ever since they wondered about the movements of the moon and the stars."

We were silent for a while. At last the Great Mother stood up.

"I've got some special goggles for you," she said, delving into her big bag. "Why don't you put them on?"

"Do I really need these?" asked Brydie, dithering a bit.

But I put mine on at once.

"These are great, Brydie. I seem to be completely part of everything around me. Go on, give them a try."

"I see what you mean," she said, putting hers on.

"Well now, I expect you're wondering why we have stopped here," said the Great Mother. "Tell me what you can see with your special goggles. They let you see things that are very, very small. But they also let you see things that are very, very big."

"I can see what look like enormous clouds of smoke drifting around," I said, "but something funny is happening."

"That's right," said the Great Mother. "What looks like smoke is really clouds of a gas called hydrogen. What is difficult for you to realise is just how big these clouds are." She thought for a while. "You probably know that light travels very fast."

"Oh yes," I said. "thirty million kilometres a second!"

"Well," said the Great Mother. "You see that cloud over there. It takes light more than a hundred thousand years to travel from one side of it to the other."

"I can see why we need these goggles," said Brydie, in total amazement.

"Each of these big clouds will evolve and form a galaxy. There are going to be more than a thousand million of them," said the Great Mother, "and they aren't just scattered about anyhow. They are grouped into vast swathes and clusters. They are the building blocks of the universe.

"What do you think of it?"

We had a good look round and tried to grasp what the Great Mother had told us. We tried to visualise the size of the clouds all round us and, at the same time, to see the tiny atoms of hydrogen. The goggles helped, but it was a struggle.

It was all so vast, so strange and we felt so small. So very small.

"If you think you're small," said the Great Mother, "try being a couple of atoms of hydrogen just for a little while."

4

The Making of a Star

---

*T*ime travellers should expect adventures but the thought of being turned into an atom and let loose in space made me distinctly nervous. I looked at Brydie – she was excited.

"It could be fun, Bran."

"What exactly will happen to us?" I asked the Great Mother. "Will you be able to find us and turn us back into ourselves? How long will it take?"

To tell the truth I was scared stiff.

"Don't be afraid, I'll keep my eye on you the whole time.

"As you are brother and sister you'll make a good molecule. That's how hydrogen likes to be. Its atoms go about in pairs.

"Hold hands and close your eyes," she said putting her own hands on our heads. "Enjoy the Dance of Hydrogen."

We felt ourselves shrinking until we were no bigger than a molecule, flying very fast through space.

"I can see another molecule alongside us," said Brydie. "I think it's pulling us sideways."

Soon more hydrogen molecules joined us and we started circling around each other.

"We are being pulled all over the place," I said.

More and more molecules joined in. One of them actually bumped into us and gave us a push. The more we bumped the faster we went and the warmer it got. We were having a lot of fun. After a while we were travelling so fast that the bumps became quite violent.

"This isn't fun any more," said Brydie.

"It's like a bad ride on the dodgems, and I'm roasting."

It was just beginning to feel really hot when, in the nick of time, the Great Mother appeared out of nowhere and we became ourselves again.

"How long have we been away?" I asked, "and what was happening to us?"

"That little trip took you about a million years," said the Great Mother. "All the pulling and bumping was caused by the force of gravity."

"But I thought there was no gravity in space," I said, "Aren't astronauts always talking about being weightless?"

"Well, they are. Nearly," replied the Great Mother. "Because, you see, everything attracts everything else in the universe. When you kick a football into the air, what happens?

"It comes down again," I replied.

"Exactly! It is attracted to the earth. In space even tiny hydrogen atoms attract each other, given enough time. Exactly why this happens is still a bit of a mystery."

"I suppose we were getting hot because of all the bumping," said Brydie.

"Yes, you were just beginning to make a star when I pulled you out. Stars get really hot."

"I hope the star can carry on without us," said Brydie.

"Let's stay here for a bit and see," she replied.

With our goggles we looked at the cloud of hydrogen that had formed around us when we were a molecule. The centre of the cloud looked very dense and it began to glow with white light.

"Is the hydrogen burning?" asked Brydie.

"In a way. But it's not like a fire burning. The hydrogen atoms are being squeezed together by gravity so much that they are joining together to make a new gas called helium. This gives off a lot of heat and that increases the pressure to balance the force of gravity. A lot of stars reach a kind of balance and can go on burning, as you would say it, for billions of years. Your sun's like that."

"Is our sun just a star like all the others?" asked Brydie.

"Of course. But no two stars are alike, they are all different.

"We now have to travel a long way forward in time, nearly nine billion years – that's almost two thirds of our journey. Then we have to try and find your galaxy, which you call the Milky Way. And, in the Milky Way we need to find a particular star called Tiamat, because something wonderful is going to happen to her."

What wonderful thing could possibly happen to a star, we wondered as we travelled on.

5

The Wonder that is Tiamat

---

*A*s we made our seemingly endless way through time we looked about us. Everywhere we could see immense galaxies being born and stars coming to life. Against the intense blackness of space there were great glowing clouds of all possible shapes and patterns and colours, more different reds and blues than I thought existed. Wherever we looked it was different. As for the stars, there were big ones and little ones, stars in twos and threes, stars in large clusters and stars on their own, millions of them.

"Isn't this wonderful, Brydie? Am I dreaming or is this really happening?"

"Stop asking difficult questions."

The Great Mother was smiling and obviously delighting in everything that was happening. We began to see the universe bursting with newness.

"I didn't know that space looked like this!" I said.

"Neither did I" said Brydie. "It's beautiful and frightening at the same time."

At last the Great Mother began to look around as if she was searching for something. We changed direction a bit as she took us towards an enormous group of galaxies.

"This is the Virgo cluster," she said. "Somewhere in here is your galaxy, the Milky Way."

She seemed to know where we were going, although how she could tell one galaxy from the other was a mystery to us.

"Here we are! This is the Milky Way," she said. "The problem is, I'm not sure where to find Tiamat. The last time I was here she hadn't been born. Look out for a very large and very bright star."

"Is that Tiamat?" asked Brydie hopefully, pointing to a star that looked much bigger and brighter then the stars nearby.

"I think you are right. Yes, that's Tiamat. Now we have to be rather careful. We shouldn't get too close. It's too dangerous. We may have to wait here a bit."

"Why? Don't you know when something is going to happen?" I asked. "We thought you knew everything, didn't we Brydie."

"I know a great deal," replied the Great Mother. "But there are many things in the universe that nobody can know. The universe needs some freedom so it can create new things. I give it that freedom. I take that risk.

"Tiamat was born from a very, very large cloud of hydrogen and she is a very large star, about fifty times larger than your sun. I know when she was born and I know more or less how long very large stars will live. But just when she'll die is another matter."

"Do you mean that this beautiful star is going to die? How can a star die? And are we going to see it happen? I'm not sure I want to," said Brydie.

"Yes, Tiamat is going to die. Of course it is a sad moment, but it is also a happy one. Tiamat will be reborn, but not as a star. Let me try to explain…"

Just as she said this there was a blinding flash and Tiamat seemed to grow until she blotted out many of the stars around her.

"It has started," cried the Great Mother. "Don't look at her for too long."

We were petrified. Tiamat went on growing and great streams and fountains of light shot out in all directions. One seemed to be heading straight for us.

"Look out!" she warned, "we'd better get out of the way."

The streams of light spread out as they shot through space and got dimmer the farther they went. After a bit things seemed to quieten down.

"That was scary," I said. "I found it exciting," said Brydie.

"You're both right," said the Great Mother. "Now it's a bit quieter I will explain what's happened. It's rather difficult, but I'll do my best.

"I've already told you about smaller stars. But, in a very big star the force of gravity squeezes a lot harder and just making helium isn't enough to get a balance. Tiamat had to go on making heavier and heavier atoms. When atoms join together to make heavier ones a lot of heat is given off and this increases the pressure at the centre of the star, pushing against the force of gravity trying to squash it.

"That's how lots of different atoms were created: carbon, oxygen, nitrogen, sulphur and calcium and many more. The end of the line was iron. When Tiamat started to make iron, that was the beginning of dying. When she had made lots of iron she could do no more to oppose the force of gravity. She just collapsed inwards and the shock caused the enormous explosion that you saw as the blinding light.

"But Great Mother," I said. "iron can't collapse, it's solid."

"You have no idea of what it's like at the centre of a large star like Tiamat," she replied. "The temperatures and pressures are absolutely enormous. The material of the star is much heavier than solid iron but it is still a gas. This may sound amazing but you'll just have to believe me.

"And now, most of the iron and carbon and oxygen and the rest have been blasted out into space as tiny flecks of dust and gas, millions and millions of tonnes of it."

"You said there was an explosion," I said. "But I didn't hear a bang."

"There's no real sound in space. There has to be something for the sound to travel through and in space there is nothing, or at least not enough to make any sound that you could hear," replied the Great Mother. "I could hear her death-cry and it was a cry of sadness for the end of her magnificent life and also a cry of joy for her future rebirth."

'You said this before Great Mother – but how is she reborn?" I asked.

"She's reborn as you and Brydie!" she replied. "You are starchildren."

"Oh!" we said together.

"It's a long story, which will take more than four billion years. We've already travelled a long way from the Very Beginning. Nearly ten billion years. I've shown you the Dance of Hydrogen. I've talked nearly enough. We'll soon meet Mother Gaia who will show you the wonders of the earth. And on the way I'll tell you the story of how Tiamat got her name.

"The story is written in a long poem. It tells of how the people of ancient Babylon thought the world came into being.

Tiamat was their goddess of the sea and, with her husband Apsu, she gave birth to a family of gods and goddesses, including a grandson called Marduk. The younger gods rebelled against their parents and killed Apsu. They then called on Marduk to fight and kill Tiamat. It was a fearsome battle. Marduk made a bow and a net in which to ensnare Tiamat. He called upon the winds to be his allies and mounted his storm chariot drawn by four horses, the Killer, the Relentless, the Trampler and the Swift. The poem tells of how Marduk challenged his grandmother Tiamat:

> Stand up, that I and you might meet in single combat!"
> When Tiamat heard this,
> She was like one possessed; she took leave of her senses.
> In fury Tiamat cried out aloud.
> To the roots her legs shook both together.
> She recited a charm, kept casting her spell,
> While the gods of battle sharpened their weapons.
> Then Tiamat and Marduk joined issue, wisest of gods.
> They strove in single combat, locked in battle.
> The lord spread out his net to enfold her,
> The Evil Wind, which followed behind, he let loose in her face.
> When Tiamat opened her mouth to consume him,
> He drove in the Evil Wind while as yet she had not shut her lips.
> As the terrible winds filled her belly,
> Her body was distended and her mouth was wide open.
> He released the arrow, it tore her belly,

31

It cut through her insides, splitting the heart.
Having thus subdued her, he extinguished her life.
He cast down her carcass to stand upon it.

"Marduk then split Tiamat's body in two. One half became the sky and the sun and the moon and the stars, and from the other half he formed the earth."

"That's a horrible story," said Brydie.

"Yes," replied the Great Mother. "But it says that creation can be difficult. It is a real struggle that can involve extreme violence. It also says that new life can only come out of a death. But come, it's time to be off. Mother Gaia is waiting for us."

6

Earth is Born

---

e hadn't travelled far when we saw someone in the distance who was waving with both hands as if we were expected.

"Is that Mother Gaia?" we both asked hopefully.

"Yes, it certainly is. It always cheers me up to see her. She's so welcoming and her hospitality is well known everywhere."

Mother Gaia greeted the Great Mother with a small bow.

"Welcome Great Mother," she said. She then turned to us and shook our hands eagerly.

"And here you are dear Brydie and Bran. I've been so looking forward to your visit."

Compared with the Great Mother, Mother Gaia was small and rather stout. She was wearing a practical sky-blue jogging suit with yellow trainers.

"Are you ready to guide us through the story of Earth?" asked the Great Mother.

"Yes, of course, I'm looking forward to it," she replied. "But first I would like us to go and look at what is left of Tiamat.

"I like to do this whenever I'm here, in remembrance and thanksgiving, because in a way she is my mother."

By now all traces of the terrific explosion had gone and all we could see was a very small circular shape that was shining but nothing like as brightly as a star.

"We can go closer, but not too close," said Mother Gaia. "You know that Tiamat collapsed by being squeezed by the force of gravity. Well, what you see here is the result. Tiamat has been reduced to a small sphere about twenty-five kilometres in diameter, but she weighs more than a million times the weight of the earth and she is spinning round fifty times a second. Her force of gravity will squash you flat if you get too close."

We all stood and looked at Tiamat and remembered her brief life of 150 million years and her spectacular death.

"Now we can go and see how she's reborn," said Mother Gaia.

"Not another long trek, please Mother Gaia," I pleaded. "All this time travelling is hard work."

"We don't have far to go," she replied. "Do you see that cloud over there, where it looks as though a star's being born?"

"Yes. Is that the sun?" asked Brydie. "Great Mother told us that our sun is a star."

"Yes. In the cloud that's giving birth to the sun is some of the dust and gas blown out from Tiamat. This soon starts circling around the sun and forming itself into a disk. Use your goggles and look at what's happening."

"I can see it swirling around the sun in great streams and clouds," I said. "But the stuff near the sun looks different from the stuff further away. And there are some places where it looks as though the stuff is gathering together."

"You're seeing the birth of the planets," said Mother Gaia. "Near to the sun it's mostly iron and rock dust. Further away it's mostly water and gasses, that's why it looks different.

"Let's take a short walk of about forty million years and see what happens. You'll be amazed, I promise."

As we walked, Mother Gaia told us to look specially at the third planet out from the sun.

"That is planet Earth," she said proudly. "So far it's just a mass of iron and rock."

We soon saw a much smaller mass collide with the earth. It was more like a slow crunch than a collision and when it was over we saw that the earth now had a small planet of its own.

"That must be the Moon," I said. "Amazing!"

Further away from the sun I could see a large planet. Compared with Earth it was enormous.

"That's planet Jupiter," said Mother Gaia. "He has a very important part to play in the story of Earth.

"You see how some of the watery stuff even further from the sun is gathering into small clumps. You know them as comets. They move round the sun but the pull of Jupiter's gravity is so strong that as they pass by, some of their orbits get changed from circles into more like ovals. Some of them can get very close to Earth.

"Look, you can see one now."

We could see a fairly large comet head almost straight for Earth.

"I think its going to collide," said Brydie. "What will happen if it does?"

It did. It made an enormous crater.

"It all looks extremely violent," said Mother Gaia. "But these collisions are bringing the water and the gasses that will in time make Earth a place where life can start."

When we finished the forty million year walk we stopped for a while.

"Everything that Earth needs is there now," said Mother Gaia. "The inside is mostly molten iron. It is very, very hot. The outside is lighter rock forming a skin over the surface. You can see where the water is gathering into large masses on the surface and forming oceans. With your goggles you can see that over the surface there is a layer of gas. It is mostly carbon dioxide. Earth is ready for life to begin. The sun will provide light and warmth for millions and millions of years."

Mother Gaia stopped talking and we just stood there silently looking. So this was Earth, at last. It was beautiful. But I felt like an alien. Home was still a very long time away.

"From now on our time travel will only follow the evolution of planet Earth," said the Great Mother.

"And we'll have a party when we get there!" said Mother Gaia.

7

The Party of the Planets

"The time has come to land on Earth," said the Great Mother. "This is an important occasion and it would be good to travel there in style."

"Let's take a ride down a sunbeam," she said. "Put your goggles on Bran and Brydie and all hold hands!"

And with this we launched ourselves into the path of a very bright beam of light coming from the young sun and heading straight for Earth. In a few minutes we arrived. It was a gentle touch-down. After so much space travel it was good to have solid ground under our feet.

We had landed close to a large log cabin.

"This is where I live when I'm not busy trying the keep the Earth in order," said Mother Gaia, opening the door, "let's go in."

We let the Great Mother lead the way as we stepped into a large, comfortably furnished room. It was obvious that some-one had lived here for a very long time.

"Feel free to have a look around," said Mother Gaia.

I immediately wondered whether the Triple Mirror could be here and decided to do a little secret looking.

There was a gentle, sweet smell of apple wood in the room coming from an old-fashioned looking stove. There were three well-worn easy chairs with colourful cushions. In one of them a hairy creature was curled up and fast asleep.

"That's Fritz. He's a racoon and keeps me company whenever I am here."

There was an odd looking map on one of the walls. It was obviously a map of the world, but I couldn't recognise anything.

"That's a map of the continent called Vendia which existed nearly six hundred million years before the Present," explained Mother Gaia. "You and Brydie will have a chance to see it later on."

By far the most striking thing in the room was the bookcase. It occupied a whole wall and stretched from floor to ceiling. It was full of books. There were also piles of books on the floor, in odd corners and even on the staircase. Lying on a sloping table was the largest book I had ever seen. It was bound in leather and was so old and tatty that I found it difficult to read the title which was embossed in gold: *Record of the Extinct Species of Plants and Animals on Planet Earth – With Illustrations.*

I decided to ask Mother Gaia about this but she was talking to Brydie. They were looking at a table covered with rocks and fossils.

"Mum would love it here, Mother Gaia," she said.

At the far end of the room I saw a table laid for a meal.

"I can see you're looking at the party table," said Mother Gaia with a smile. "Everything's ready."

"You're in charge here Mother Gaia," said the Great Mother. "We're certainly hungry and thirsty so your idea seems excellent."

We both nodded. We took off our boots and goggles, spruced ourselves up and were invited to the table. It was round and set for six and was filled with lots of delicious looking goodies. There were sticky buns, pizza bites, mini-pancakes, moon babies, chocolate fingers, marzipan apples and Jupiter jellies. In the centre of the table stood the Gaia surprise cake. What a selection! Not to forget the Venus water that Mother

Gaia poured for us. However, before we started to eat we were asked if we would like to invite a friend each.

"Oh, yes please," said Brydie without losing an instant. "Could I have Amber? She's my rabbit."

No sooner had she said it than there was Amber, sitting on three cushions on the chair next to her. I had to do some quick thinking because I don't have many friends. So I thought of an animal too: a bird perhaps. I asked for a raven. In a flash a raven was sitting on an upturned cardboard box on the chair next to me.

"You may call me Corax," said the raven.

The party was complete and we started tucking in. Amber had a good bowl of greenery and Corax ate small meat balls from his special dish. There was soft music all round us, and all six of us were having a good time.

There were planet poppers for everyone. These were like

Christmas crackers. Inside each one was a paper hat, a chocolate in a wrapper and a riddle. We worked hard at the riddles. It turned out that the answers were the names of the planets!

We ate a lot. Brydie was allowed to cut the cake. It was a lemon cake. Hidden in the middle was vanilla ice-cream with small sweet strawberries.

Mother Gaia suggested that we might say something about our names.

"I'll start with mine," she said. "Gaia or Mother Earth was the name given to me by some of the early people who lived in Greece. They believed that the earth was a living thing, like a person. Recently people are beginning to call the earth Gaia again. I am really touched by it."

"Now Bran and Brydie, tell us about your names," said the Great Mother.

I was happy to go first: talking about ourselves was easy. Dad had often told us about our names. So I began.

"Brydie and I have Irish names. Dad read me the story of Bran from a long poem called 'The Voyage of Bran MacFerbal'. Shall I tell it to you?

"One evening, Bran is walking on his land. He hears enchanting music and falls asleep. When he wakes up there's a beautiful blossoming apple branch beside him. That night the Goddess comes to his castle with another apple branch. She sings, and in the song she invites him to come to the Other-world where people live forever.

"The Otherworld is one of a group of islands far in the west towards the setting sun. Bran sets sail with twenty-seven friends to find this land. They have many adventures but they finally find the Land of Women, where Bran meets the Goddess again. When they want to return home they are told that this is not possible as hundreds of years have passed, though only one year seemed to have passed for them on the island.

"In spite of the warning they set sail for home but they have to sail the seas for ever because if they set foot on Irish soil they would all crumble into dust.

"Well done Bran!" said Mother Gaia. "What about your name Brydie?"

"There were two famous women called Bridget or Brydie," she began. "One was the Celtic Saint Bridget of Kildare. She was known for her generosity. Hungry people came to her abbey and always received food and shelter. Her larder was never empty, people said. There was a holy fire at the abbey which never went out and was attended by twenty nuns. With Saint Patrick she is the patron saint of Ireland.

"But there was another Bridget who was widely honoured before Christian missionaries came to Ireland. She was the Celtic goddess of fire, in the home and in the smithy. She was also goddess of poets and prophets, healers and midwives."

"She also had a mirror in which she could sometimes see the future and the wolf was one of her animals," added Mother Gaia. "I think Akka's message was specially for you Brydie."

"How did you know about Akka?" I asked. "Do you know where we can find the Triple Mirror?"

"I know many things that have happened," she replied, "But I do not know where the mirror will be when it lets you find it."

So it wasn't here then.

I suddenly remembered reading about space travel and how time passed differently. I had a really urgent question. "Our Journey of Wonders is rather like the Voyage of Bran, isn't it? Will Brydie and I be able to go home when it's over?" We both looked anxiously at the Great Mother for her answer.

"Trust me. All will be well," she replied. "The journey we are on is very like the 'Voyage of Bran'. You will be changed by your adventure and the world will seem different to you, but I promise to get you home safely!"

Brydie and I looked at each other with relief.

Then Brydie asked, "Mother Gaia, why does the goddess give Bran branches of apple blossom?"

"Let me see – in the Celtic world apple trees and apples were a sign of abundance. Apple trees and apples ask us to open our hearts more fully so we will receive more. Our true power lies in giving of ourselves in open hearted generosity."

We all looked at the Great Mother. Would she say anything about her name?

"The people of the Earth have given me many names. But my true name is known only to myself," she said firmly.

"But you two have beautiful names," she continued. "Let us now drink to the birth of the planets of the solar system."

Our glasses were filled with Venus water and we drank.

"We drink especially to the birth of planet Earth," we both said.

"Of course, little earthlings. And I drink to the sun who makes life possible on planet Earth."

We were all becoming quite merry and I wondered what Venus water was. It tasted of honey and was certainly delicious. Amber jumped off her cushions and started to hop around. Corax left his box, flapping his wings and chased Amber. Suddenly we were all on our feet. We heard some music start up. "Let's do the Dance of Hydrogen," suggested Brydie. Everyone joined in, even the animals. First we danced far away from each other then we came closer and closer until we could hardly move. "Now we are a star," I exclaimed. "The mystery of gravity has pulled us together." We did the dance several times. We could try it at our discos at home.

Soon it was time to leave the cabin and continue our journey through time. We pulled on our yellow boots, picked up our goggles and were about to leave when I had a brilliant idea. "Can we take Corax and Amber with us, Great Mother?" I asked.

"Why not," she replied. "Brydie can carry Amber and Corax can ride on your shoulder."

8

The First Bubbles of Life

We hadn't travelled very far when Mother Gaia found a good place to stop. It was close to the sea. Looking inland we could see extinct volcanoes with their great lava flows now turned into solid rock. In the far distance two active volcanoes were billowing clouds of steam and dust. There was a sharp smell of sulphur in the air. There wasn't a blade of grass, or plant, or tree of any kind, just bare rock. The sky was very bright and the sun was blisteringly hot. It was a weird sort of place. Mother Gaia opened her rucksack and pulled out Mexican style sun hats for us to put on.

"Let's walk to that shallow lagoon over there. You'll find no footpaths here, so watch how you go."

We made slow progress as we clambered over the rocks. We had hardly started when panic struck. Corax, who had been sitting quietly on my shoulder, suddenly flew off and was soon out of sight. Oh no, I thought, will I ever see him again?

"Not to worry, Bran. He just wants to stretch his wings. He'll be back. There is nothing for him to eat here or anywhere else on this naked earth."

We reached the lagoon. The water was very calm and a beautiful transparent blue.

"This looks great for a swim!" I said.

"Yes please," begged Brydie, looking at Mother Gaia.

"Sorry, but that won't be possible. The water is far too hot, you would be scalded."

I was feeling depressed for the first time on The Great Journey of Wonders. Lots of travelling, too much 'look and learn', and now Corax gone and to top it all, no swimming.

"I am not sure that I like it here, Mother Gaia," said Brydie.

"I know, it's not very inviting," she replied. "But this is where life begins. That's why we are here, to take a closer look at this lagoon."

"Are we going to see the beginning of life?"

"I'm not sure it is possible to say that life had a beginning," replied Mother Gaia. "You could say that it began at the Very Beginning, or that it began with the death of Tiamat, or that it began on Earth."

This made us think about the kind of a journey we were on. We realised that it was made of lots of little journeys that didn't begin or end because they were all parts of one big journey.

"It's going to be really difficult to show you what's happening," said Mother Gaia. "What you would call life will begin when the earth is about six hundred million years old and it will happen in a shallow part of the sea.

"But first of all let's try to find some of the things that are struggling to come alive: the explorers or pioneers. "

"Carbon is the key to life," she continued,. "the carbon produced in the death of Tiamat which was swept up in the birth of the solar system and the birth of Earth. Carbon is special. It can join up with itself and with hydrogen and oxygen and nitrogen and other elements to form lots of chemicals that are chains and loops and all sorts of different shapes.

"Look into the water and see if you can see anything. Use your goggles to see small – very small."

I looked very hard. There was certainly a lot happening but it was very difficult to see any kind of pattern. I could see tiny twiggy things and they were joining up and breaking apart and twisting and turning. But everything looked all mixed up, rather like home-made soup. At last, Brydie spotted something different.

"I think I can see places where the twiggy things seem to be inside what look like little bubbles."

"What you are seeing are things trying to come alive," said Mother Gaia. "What's going on inside the oily bubbles is twiggy carbon things changing into different twiggy carbon things. Because it's happening inside a bubble the changes become more organised. Some of the bubbles are taking bits from outside and turning them into more of the bits that are inside. This means that the bubbles get bigger. In the end the bubble gets too big and it divides into two smaller bubbles. But there is no way of being sure that both parts of the bubble contain all that is needed to go on making more of itself."

"What makes all this happen?" I asked. "Are you doing it Mother Gaia? "

"Certainly not! It happens by itself because this is the way things are. The universe is endlessly creative.

"To become life as we know it, these little bubbles have two problems to solve. I told you that they have to take in some of the carbon bits they need through the skin of the bubble. These are very special bits and they will soon be used up. The bubbles have to work out how to make more of themselves inside and only bring in simpler bits from outside, from their environment. And also they have to find a way of making sure that when the bubble divides all the necessary bits are passed on to each bubble. The hard thing is solving both problems at the same time. It'll take millions of years."

"Millions of years!" said Brydie. "I thought we would see it all here."

"There is plenty of time. Great Mother has seen to that."

As we stood looking into the lagoon, I heard a flapping of wings and there was Corax looking very hot and breathless. He looked at the water in the lagoon but soon he realised that it was too hot to drink.

"Oh Corax." We couldn't help laughing. It was such a relief to see him again.

"Let's stay here at this lagoon but move on in time," suggested the Great Mother, who had been quietly watching.

This we did.

"Let's walk over there," she said, pointing to a quiet corner of the lagoon. "Can you see anything? It'll be very small."

"Where, where? I can't see a thing," I said.

"Neither can I," said Brydie. "Oh, now I think I do. Look – just by that small reddish stone."

There, sure enough, was a tiny glistening roundish something, which as we watched, grew longer and then divided into two. And, spellbound, we watched as each of these slowly grew and then grew longer and then divided again into two. Now there were four.

"You have witnessed the birth of Life," said the Great Mother proudly. "You see, endless little bubbles have tried and failed. This one has become a little personality. It can organise itself really well. It can take in nourishment from outside for energy and growth, through a network of chemical reactions. It also knows how to get rid of its waste products. It can make excellent copies of itself. Some may be slightly different, but this may be useful in helping them to survive in a changing environment. This is the way all life as we know it will work."

I took Brydie's hand and gave it a squeeze. We saw the Great Mother wipe away a tear.

"You knew about this, Great Mother!" exclaimed Mother Gaia. "You knew you could bring us to the right place at just the right time. Life is on its way! We have something to celebrate. The possibility present at the Very Beginning has at last become a reality. And as it so happens I do have a bottle of champagne in my rucksack. I thought it might come in useful sometime. Do you think on this very special occasion Bran and Brydie might be allowed to join us in a toast?"

"Well, just a small glass, perhaps," replied the Great Mother.

The cork popped very satisfyingly and flew up into the air. Corax took off and managed to catch it before it fell into the lagoon.

"Well done Corax!" said Mother Gaia. "We don't want to disturb our precious living creature at this delicate time, do we?"

We raised our glasses. "To Life!"

We took a last look at the lagoon and got ready to continue our journey with Corax and Amber.

"We're going to meet some inventors," said Mother Gaia mysteriously.

9

We Meet the Early Inventors

It was pouring with rain when we touched down on Earth again. What a welcome after a good four hundred million years of travelling! We were all getting thoroughly soaked, including Corax and Amber.

"My beautiful yellow boots are getting all squelchy," I grumbled.

The landscape around us was as barren as before and now it was wet as well. There were mountains in the distance but they were half hidden in mist and cloud. The only good thing was that the air was warm.

"Not to worry," said Mother Gaia, cheerily. "It'll soon clear up. Let's start walking. The sea is less than ten minutes away from here."

"Is that where we're meeting the inventors?" I asked not seeing any around where we were.

"Yes it is," she said not giving anything more away.

I looked at Brydie, wondering what to make of it. The rocky ground underfoot was slippery and we made slow progress.

"You see, rain is good news here," said Mother Gaia. "Evaporation from the sea makes clouds which then make rain on the land. Rain, sun and wind all slowly break up the rocks into sand and clay which are swept into rivers and carried down to the sea where they provide food for the inventors."

I looked at Brydie again. Who were these inventors? We trudged on in the rain although it was beginning to look a lot clearer.

Suddenly Brydie shouted, "Oh look, a rainbow. Isn't it fantastic!"

We all stopped and stared. It was the most perfect half circle rainbow I had ever seen.

"Look, there is a fainter second rainbow outside the first. How wonderful." Brydie was ecstatic.

My grumbles were forgotten. We had arrived at the sea shore. It looked as though the tide was out. The sun was now beating down on our backs and soon we were all steaming. The sun must be really strong here.

"Let's go and have a look," said Mother Gaia. "Do you see those dark green things in the shallows that look rather like large cushions? Let's wade out there for a closer look. That is where the inventors are."

"How about Amber and Corax," asked Brydie.

"We can leave them here, they'll be alright."

At last it dawned on me that we weren't looking for people but for some other inventive life form!

"Yes, these are the inventors, you know them as bacteria," said Mother Gaia.

"Bacteria!" we both exclaimed. What could they possibly invent?

"These cushiony things are colonies of enormous numbers of bacteria, but very special ones, very different from the first living creature," began Mother Gaia. "Some of them have invented how to use energy from the sun. That's what the green is for, it's called chlorophyll. It traps sunlight, and using water and carbon dioxide these bacteria can make nearly all that they need inside themselves. They don't need much special food; they can live almost anywhere where there is water and light. It's a fantastic invention.

"As you can see, nothing can live on the land yet," she went on. "If you look at the green cushions you will see that they're giving off tiny little bubbles of gas. It's oxygen, and in tens of millions of years this will provide enough oxygen in the air to make a layer of ozone, which is a kind of oxygen, high in the atmosphere to shield the land from ultra-violet light. Only then will life be possible on the land."

"Wow, we didn't know that bacteria were so important, did we Brydie? "

"It was very clever of these bacteria to work out how to live as they do. It took them a long time. As the Great Mother said, it's been about four hundred million years since life began and for another six hundred million years bacteria will be the only living creatures. That's a very long time. The bacteria are exploring different ways of living, either making the things they need or taking them from other bacteria."

"That doesn't seem to be a very friendly thing to do," said Brydie.

"It's what you do," said Mother Gaia. "Just about everything you eat has been made by other living things."

"Yes, I suppose so," she replied. "I hadn't thought of it like that."

I was ready for more action. "Could we go for a swim here," I asked. "We're damp already and our clothes will dry quicker if we lay them out on the rocks."

"I don't see why not," replied Mother Gaia. "But you mustn't touch the green cushions and please stay close by. There is practically no oxygen in the air here and the Great Mother is making it possible for you to breathe. It's very hard work for her if you get too far away."

In no time we were in the water and swimming around, taking care not to go too far. The water was really warm. It was great. I stuck my head under water to take a closer look at one of the green cushions when, suddenly, I felt myself shrinking. It went on and on. I was inside the cushion. There just in front of me was one of the green bacteria. It was obviously dead. Others cells had grown on top of it and cut it off from the light. Something inside me told me that it would be good to eat. Once it was inside me I found that there were some bits of it that were no use, so I pushed them out. Straight away there was another cell (was it Brydie, I wondered) which found them good to eat. I realised that all round me were different bacteria eating things that other bacteria couldn't use. Nothing was being wasted or thrown away.

I was just beginning to get used to my new life when along came a particularly large cell which looked as though it was going to eat me! Help! But as soon as it got close enough to be dangerous I found myself in human shape again, swimming like mad for the shore. And there was Brydie doing the same.

"You had to learn what it's like to be bacteria. They're really important and if I'd suggested it you would have said no," said Mother Gaia so calmly that we couldn't be cross with her for playing a trick on us.

"I've always thought that bacteria were nasty things," said Brydie. "They make people ill and food go bad."

"I know that on your TV there are lots of ads trying to sell you things that kill bacteria," said Mother Gaia. "But very few bacteria are what you would call harmful. Most of them are very useful. In fact, without bacteria life on Earth would not be possible. They do most of the recycling.

"It's time to move on. This'll be another longish trip. We'll see things that you'll recognise as animals and plants."

"Good," I said. "It's about time that Corax and Amber had some company."

"I don't know about that," replied Mother Gaia. "Where we're going to next, all the animals live in the sea."

As we got ready to leave we looked around for Corax and Amber, but Amber was nowhere to be seen. While we were having our adventure with the bacteria, she had vanished. Brydie called out her name several times without success. Then she had a brilliant idea of singing one of her songs:

Life is like a crystal in the sun,
We're all just colours of the rainbow.

I knew the song very well and so did Amber, but nothing stirred anywhere. Brydie began to cry. I didn't know what to do and was about to ask Mother Gaia for help when Corax flew off. He landed on a rock some distance away and started cawing and flapping his wings.

"That must be it," Brydie said excitedly. "Corax is telling us where to look."

I scrambled over the rocks as fast as I could and found Amber who was burrowing happily in a patch of sand. Triumphantly I gave Amber back to Brydie, who scolded her for running off like that. Oh! what a relief.

With Corax perched on my shoulder, we quickly rejoined the Great Mother and Mother Gaia.

"Why don't we pay a flying visit to Scotland?"

"Yes, why not Mother Gaia," said the Great Mother.

And off we went.

10

Looking for Nessie Again

---

e were time travelling high above the earth again. I was in a happy mood and looking forward to our next landing. Mother Gaia had promised that we were going to see Scotland as well as some animals in the sea. Putting two and two together it seemed to me that there was a good chance of finding Nessie. But I had some serious doubts and so it seemed did Brydie.

"Mother Gaia," she asked. "How do bacteria evolve into dinosaurs?"

"That's not a simple question, Brydie," she chuckled, "but a good one I admit.

"Now, let me see. Where shall I begin? What you saw in the green cushions were bacteria co-operating with each other so that nothing was wasted. What happens is that some of them find themselves inside a larger cell, but stay alive. That way they form a new unit which can go off by itself. It doesn't have to stay inside the cushion.

"If you were a single bacterial cell and you had two different living bacteria inside you, one that could make sugar using energy from the sun, like the green ones, and another one which used the energy from sugar to produce growth, that's obviously an advantage. You have more happening inside you and you need less from outside. That's more or less what happened. The result was a new kind of organism which, in turn, evolved into lots of different creatures.

"Most of them are very small. Some of them are very beautiful and some, which you know as seaweeds, can get quite big. These new creatures together with the bacteria are the only forms of life for more than three thousand million years."

"Really!" said Brydie.

"I'm sorry Brydie, we are arriving. The rest of the answer will have to wait."

We stayed high above the earth. As we looked down all we could see was one enormous area of dry land surrounded by ocean, a sort of super-continent.

The Great Mother and Mother Gaia were having a bit of an argument. Finally, they seemed to agree.

"We want to show you the land that will become Scotland," said the Great Mother. "We're having to think backwards from where it will be in the Present to where it is now, if you see what we mean. It's not easy."

"I don't get it, don't you know where Scotland is?" I asked. "It can't have moved all that much."

"Yes it can," said Mother Gaia. "Do you remember the map hanging on the wall of my cabin?

"Yes, you said it was a map of Vendia," I replied.

"Well, that is what you are seeing down there. And at the moment we're just about over the South Pole. Vendia will slowly break up. That bit of land down there (she pointed) will become Scotland north of the Great Glen and that bit over there (she pointed a long way away) will be south of the Great Glen. But a lot will happen between now and then.

"You mean that Scotland will move all the way from the South Pole!" I exclaimed.

"Yes, it's hard to believe isn't it," said the Great Mother.

"Can we go down and take a look? I want to tell Mum and Dad that Brydie and I stood on Scotland's bed rock."

We quickly zoomed down and walked around for a while. I felt like a complete stranger. The silence was unbearable. I had to believe it was Scotland, but not as we knew it. All we could see was just one vast boulder field. It reminded me of the summit of Scafell Pike which I had climbed last year with my cousins.

"We won't stay here long," said Mother Gaia. "As you can see there's very little life on the land. Only a few patches of green bacteria in damp places."

Yes, it was obvious that this was no place for Nessie.

"And now we're going to where England will be. You see, at the moment it's still at the bottom of the sea."

Well! The Great Mother did say we were on a Journey of Wonders, but all this was just unbelievable.

We soon arrived at yet another sea-shore where it was a pleasant summer's day.

"Here we are. Let's go and have a look at some animals."

"I'll stay here," said the Great Mother, "and look after Amber and Corax."

We moved down into the sea. It was strange at first, but we found that we could still breathe easily. One of the Great Mother's gifts, we supposed.

What a sight! The water was beautifully clear and we could see the bottom easily. There was a lot of seaweed, but it took us some time to recognise anything like the animals we had seen in the aquarium on holiday in Plymouth. There were lots of pink things that looked like jellyfish. These seemed to be the only creatures that were actually swimming. There were some animals that looked like dark blue lobsters, but only just. There were many other strange creatures that crawled around on the bottom. To tell the truth I was pretty scared, but it didn't stop me looking for Nessie.

"I think those yellow things over there are sponges," said Brydie. "But I don't see any fish."

"You are quite right Brydie," said Mother Gaia. "There'll be no fish for another hundred million years, and even then they'll be very different from those you know.

"There is an animal around that will evolve into the fishes, but it is very small and looks more like a worm than a fish."

Mother Gaia was anxious to move on.

"It is hard work for the Great Mother to let you breathe under water," she said. "She won't be able to keep it up for much longer."

So we said good bye to these beautiful creatures and made for the shore. We all sat down on the beach near the Great Mother. While the sun dried us off Mother Gaia produced some good looking doughnuts from her rucksack. Brydie fed some small bits to the animals. We were all happy and relaxed.

"Life has been evolving for three thousand million years and only now do we see any real animals and they're all in the sea. Sorry about Nessie, Bran, but you'll have to wait another three hundred million years before Nessie and her cousins can appear."

"Now can you tell us where these animals came from?" asked Brydie.

"They evolved from one of the groups of single celled creatures. What happened is that instead of staying as separate cells some of them joined up to form colonies. Then, in the colonies, some of the cells began to take on particular jobs such as eating and moving. The cells stopped doing everything for themselves but did special things for the colony as a whole. This opened up lots of new opportunities for exploring new ways of living. You have just seen some of the results, and you will see more of the story as we travel along."

I was impatient to be off again. "Where do we go next?" I asked.

"We're going to take a look at Laurentia."

"Laurentia!" we both exclaimed.

This startled Amber so much that she jumped out of Brydie's arms and hopped away as fast as she could.

"Oh, no you don't," said Brydie as she leapt after her.

"Come here you rascal."

Amber was soon recaptured but Brydie seemed to be limping quite badly.

"My ankle hurts, I must have sprained it."

Oh no, I thought, what now?

11

From the Sea to the Land

---

e all stood round Brydie who was sitting on the beach looking miserable. It put a damper on our happy explorations under the sea. Mother Gaia gently pulled off her boot and bandaged the swollen ankle tightly while the Great Mother produced some of her delicious apple juice, "for the patient."

"Time heals," she said. "And I have plenty of time. Let's make our way to the Explorer, which is waiting just over the dunes."

Supported by Mother Gaia, Brydie hobbled along while I carried Amber. The Explorer turned out to be a round wooden platform with sturdy railings. As soon as we were all on board we took off and in a few seconds we were high above the earth.

"The Explorer will give our feet a rest," said the Great Mother, "and do the time travelling for us as well as taking us round Earth. It will give Brydie's ankle a chance to heal quickly."

Brydie and I stared in amazement at the earth below.

"Is there always as much ocean as this?" I asked.

"It varies a bit," replied Mother Gaia. "But yes, most of the time about three-quarters of the surface of Earth is seas and oceans.

"We've come up here to have a look at some of the movements of the continents. They are a vital part of Earth's journey. I know that your Mum told you something about Laurentia. I thought we'd follow it on some of its wanderings from near the South Pole as far as the Equator. A journey of two hundred and fifty million years. At the same time we have to move around the earth. I want to stay fairly high so that we can see what's happening on the big scale. We can go down for a closer look when we reach the equator."

As we hovered high over Vendia, we saw a big bit of it break away from the rest.

"Is that Laurentia, Mother Gaia?" asked Brydie.

"Good guess, Brydie."

As we travelled, Laurentia seemed to glide effortlessly across a vast ocean. We could see what looked like wrinkles coming and going especially on the north edge; and all round the edges areas seemed to dip down into the ocean for some time and then re-emerge. Also we could clearly see patches of green and reddish brown gradually spreading across the whole continent.

"Look, life is moving onto the land," said Mother Gaia. "Those coloured patches are bacteria and algae and other more complicated plants, like the mosses and liverworts that live in the Present.

"The wrinkles you see are mountain ranges being pushed up as Laurentia moves. There are active volcanoes and big earthquakes. It isn't as easy and peaceful as it looks."

We looked back to see the even bigger continent that we had left behind when we started to follow Laurentia. It was still sitting more or less over the South Pole. As we looked we saw a fairly small long piece break away from it, followed by another larger bit. Both of them seemed to be following us. After a while the smaller piece disappeared.

"What's happened to it?" asked Brydie.

"It's still there and still moving," said Mother Gaia. "It's going to be under water for a few million years. It's called Avalonia and quite soon it'll collide with Laurentia and break some bits off it that will form Scotland. The main bit of Avalonia will become the rest of Britain. The larger piece is called Baltica. And it will become most of Europe."

We saw Avalonia rise up out of the sea.

"Look, it's crashing into Laurentia – Baltica is joining in as well," I said excitedly. "Look Brydie, look at those cracks in Laurentia. One of them must be the Great Glen."

We saw it all happen in five minutes, but Mother Gaia told us that it really took several million years.

"So you see that Britain consists of bits of Laurentia and a bit of Avalonia," she explained.

"These moving continents are a puzzle," said Brydie. "Everything seems to be always on the move."

"You're absolutely right," said the Great Mother. "Galaxies, stars, planets, continents, mountains, rivers, forests, plants, animals and people – they're all on the move in their own ways.

"I think it's time to go down and have a closer look," she continued.

"We'll have to be careful about where we land. I don't want to land on a mountain. We need to have a closer look at the plants. A lot of the lower ground is very boggy."

We hovered about looking for somewhere that was dry enough for us to stand on. Mother Gaia pointed to a ridge of land that looked as though it might do.

The Explorer made a gentle landing. It was good to be on solid ground again, even though it was so hot we could hardly breathe. It looked as if it had been raining. There was a lot of mist everywhere and we couldn't see very far. What we could see were trees, at least they looked like trees but not at all like any trees that we had ever seen. They had tall trunks without branches, rather like palm trees, but the leaves were very different. Brydie walked to the nearest one and hugged it and shouted: "I love trees, lots of trees" and she started to sing one of her songs. It was really moving in that weird landscape. In order to move around we clambered over fallen trunks covered in mosses and lichens. Everywhere there were strange looking plants.

We stopped. Apart from the dripping of water the forest was completely silent.

"Why is it so quiet?" I asked in a whisper.

"Because there aren't any animals yet that can make noises. No birds or mammals. The dinosaurs are the first animals to talk to each other but there won't be any of those for another forty million years," replied Mother Gaia.

"Why don't I see any flowers?" I asked.

"There'll be no flowers for millions of years yet," said Mother Gaia.

Just then there was a whirring noise and an enormous thing like a pale green dragonfly flew past. I couldn't help ducking down as I thought it was flying straight at me.

"What was that!" I cried in alarm.

"That was the ancestor of your dragonflies," replied Mother Gaia. "There are quite a few insects about. They emerged some time ago, and in this heat they can grow quite big."

"There are also some snails and, of course, worms in the soil, but not many animals have made it onto the land yet. There's one we must try and find if we can. It spends a lot of its time in water but it can move around on dry land quite easily."

With some difficulty Mother Gaia led us down towards a large pond. There, right in front of us, with only its head out of water, was a beautiful, bright yellow and black creature, glistening with life.

I tried to get really close, tripped over a fallen log and fell headlong into the pond. The water was full of twigs, dead leaves and other horrible bits I didn't like to think about. The water was not deep. My feet soon found the soft bottom and I managed to struggle out, but I was wet through. Everyone stood there laughing at me, even Corax and Amber were positively grinning.

"I thought this might happen," said the Great Mother, "The problem is how are we to get you dry. I think we'll take a quick trip into the Permian."

"Yes, why not!" said Mother Gaia.

"What's the Permian?" asked Brydie, mystified.

"It's the name given by humans to a period in the history of Earth," replied the Great Mother. "Everything here is wet and swampy. But, in about thirty million years things get much dryer. We'll just stop long enough to get Bran dry."

It seemed no time at all before we found ourselves in a desert. The sun was very hot and my clothes were soon dry.

"Mother Gaia, what was that animal in the pond?" I asked. "It vanished under water as soon as I fell in and I didn't get a good look at it."

"The nearest thing in the Present is a newt," she replied. "But this one was much bigger than any newt you'll see. It belongs to a group which are the first animals with backbones to come on land and, like newts and frogs and toads, they have to return to fresh water to lay their eggs. That was fine in the period when we met them – there were plenty of ponds and wet places. But now it's much drier and it's difficult for them to find places to breed. But they evolved, and some of their descendants started producing eggs with leathery waterproof shells that can survive in dry places.

"Come and have a look over here."

We followed Mother Gaia to a patch of loose sand between some reddish rocks. As we watched the sand seemed to move and several small animals emerged looking rather like fat lizards.

"Their mother buried her eggs in the sand and just let the heat of the sun work on them and get them to develop," she said. Corax was, of course, extremely interested in what he saw wriggling in the sand and I had to hold him very firmly with both hands. "These baby lizards will grow to more than a metre long. They're one of the very first reptiles. Can you guess what they will evolve into?"

"You mean, this is the beginning of the dinosaurs?" I asked.

"Yes, the descendants of these animals will be the main land animals for about two hundred and fifty million years. But I can see that you know a lot about them already."

"If that is so," said the Great Mother. "I think we will skip the dinosaurs and move on to see a rather important event. Also, there is someone waiting there whom I want you to meet."

"Won't we see any dinosaurs at all?" I asked in despair.

"Don't worry," replied the Great Mother. And with that assurance we set off once again wondering where we were going and who we were going to meet.

12

The Green Man

$\mathcal{A}$ nasty surprise awaited us. Earth was no longer the radiant blue-green planet which had greeted us earlier.

"What's going on Mother Gaia? The Earth looks so weird," said Brydie.

"What's that dirty brown fog all around her?" I asked.

"We're all upset," she replied. "Just a few months ago a small asteroid collided with Earth. It landed in the sea just off what is now the Yucatan Peninsula in Mexico. The collision produced massive amounts of dust and smoke. Fires have done terrific damage. So did wind and waves. Let's go and see."

We zoomed in. Mother Gaia had to search quite a while before she found a landing place which turned out to be a large rocky ledge overlooking a valley below us.

"This fog is making life difficult for everything," she said looking anxiously around.

"Where on earth is the Green Man? He has only sixty-five million years to travel from the Present. I particularly want you two to meet him."

Then we heard a loud voice. "I'm here Mother Gaia! Sorry to be a little late. These days I am much in demand again by humans."

And there suddenly standing in front of us was the oddest person we had ever seen. He was wearing a dark green costume of ivy and oak leaves all sewn together. There were leaves in his hair and leaves growing out of his ears and nose. Maybe he came straight from a TV show.

"I am popular with artists and writers," he continued. "And recently I've been swamped by ecologists and the like who find my message inspiring."

"What is your message?" we asked, trying hard to suppress a mild attack of giggling.

"Well, what do you see?" he asked pointing to himself.

"We see leaves and a face," we replied.

"That's why I'm called the Green Man. My greenery represents nature and my face is the face of every human," he said. "You see, I'm a picture, a symbol of rebirth and renewal. I live in the human soul and reappear to warn and help in time of trouble."

The Great Mother continued, "the Green Man sums up the harmony which ought to be maintained between humanity and nature. He transmits wisdom. But, enough of that, let's look at the scene around us."

"Yes, let's see what we can see," said the Green Man. "Use your goggles. This fog is not helping us."

It was obvious that we were in for a bit of a look and learn. So I thought I had better volunteer.

"The brown fog is everywhere. It is pretty cold. The sun is blocked out and I see great animals – they're dinosaurs! There's a large herd of them blundering around in the valley and making a lot of noise. Look, one is collapsing. The conifer trees look miserable too – lost their green colour. All the ferns are wilting, they are all sick."

"So, things are not looking too good," said the Green Man. "And you Brydie?"

"Well, I'm looking at that swamp on the left," said Brydie. "I see horsetails, you can find the same kind in the Present. I see some beautiful dragonflies and two terrapins. And I think I see a small creature which looks a bit like a rat, only it isn't. It looks healthy but it's not enjoying the smog."

"Look at that big dinosaur, Brydie, isn't it a *Tyrannosaurus*? It's chasing something. It's got stuck in the swamp and it doesn't look as if it can get out."

"Yes, it's the end of a long and happy time for the dinosaurs," said the Green Man. "The first ones were no bigger than a cat. They evolved over two hundred million years to produce many different species.

"Life is suffering terribly. All the dinosaurs are dying, and lots of other plants and animals as well. But life is irrepressible. After death comes rebirth. You simply can't buck the life force."

"Like dandelions struggling up through the tarmac," interrupted Brydie.

"Something like that," replied the Green Man with a smile. "That creature you thought was a rat, Brydie, will dig a hole for itself and hide underground until things get better. It is easier for small creatures to survive, they can find shelter. Trees and plants can survive as seeds or grow again from roots deep underground where they are protected. This fog is not the worst. It will get very cold because the sunshine cannot reach the earth. But the fog will clear. Earth will recover. What was a disaster for the dinosaurs becomes an opportunity for the survivors. They'll adapt and diversify in a spectacular way and give rise, over millions of years mind you, to all the creatures of the modern world.

"What we see here is that there is a vital rule at work producing lots of different animals and plants," said the Great Mother. "It's not fixed beforehand, nor is it by pure chance, but in a kind of drift towards greater complexity and awareness. I make this possible. It is the divine creative principle.

"This is all rather difficult for you children to understand, but you'll remember my words and understand them when you're older."

I thought this might be a good time to ask the question I had been wanting to ask for a long time. "Mother Gaia, you know that enormous book in your cabin? Do you know how many extinct species there are?

"Ah, you mean the Roll of Honour. I don't think we have ever counted them, but it's possible to make a rough guess. The average life of a species is about five million years. Lots of species live for less than that, but quite a few live a lot longer. There are very roughly ten million species alive at any one time and for animals and plants this has been going on for nearly six hundred million years. That works out to well over a billion extinct species."

"A billion!" we both gasped. "That's why the book is so big!"

"I have loved and enjoyed all of them," said the Great Mother.

"Is there a chance of a monster in Loch Ness, Green Man?" I asked.

"Sorry. Most unlikely," he replied. "But people will go on looking. People live by stories of the imagination. For them Nessie will always be there. You see I'm a person of the imagination. "

"Come, let's move on to High Point," said Mother Gaia. "There we'll find refreshment."

13

A Ceremony in the Forest

*A*fter a journey of some 60 million years, a wonderful sight met our eyes. From a distance it looked like a shiny white castle in a forest, but when we got nearer we realised that it was a large white rock on which stood what looked like a small, round, Greek temple. There was a circle of stone columns supporting a domed roof. There was white furniture, a low round table and six stools. The temple was decorated with white and yellow garlands. So this was High Point. Surely the Triple Mirror was somewhere in the temple. Wasn't that the kind of place where sacred objects were kept? It would come to us, Mother Gaia had told us, so I said nothing but I was hopeful. Akka the wolf and all her friends needed our help.

"Wow! Bran, what's all this for?" said Brydie. "Do you think there's going to be another party?"

"There's going to be a ceremony here," said the Green Man, "a celebration of the universe."

We all entered the temple, Mother Gaia leading the way.

"Welcome to High Point, Brydie and Bran."

"Where exactly are we, Mother Gaia?"

"While we followed Laurentia, do you remember that there was another very large continent that we left behind at the South Pole? It's now called Gondwana and it's also moved northwards and split into two, making Africa and South America. We had to include one visit to it on our journey. We're now in the bit that became Africa."

"If you'll excuse me," said the Great Mother. "I'll go and refresh myself." And with that she disappeared. While we were waiting for her, Mother Gaia invited us to have a good look round. The view in all directions was stunning. This was another of the Great Mother's wonders. We were in the middle of

a very beautiful tropical forest. There was a lot of noise from birds and monkeys in the taller trees. Brydie saw a leopard slowly climb down a tree. I spotted several snakes. There were red, blue and green parrots. There were a lot of strange looking flowers. For the first time in my life I saw a real chameleon.

"Look over there, Bran, there's something hiding in the bushes."

"That's an okapi," said Mother Gaia. "It's very shy."

In a small clearing nearby we saw a group of strange looking chimpanzees. Some of them were trying to stand up on their hind legs.

"Look, isn't that big one using a sharp stone as a tool," said Brydie.

"I see that a lot of the animals look a bit different from the ones we know," I said. "Why is that Mother Gaia?"

"Well, High Point is not the Present, we still have about five million years to go," she replied. "But it's a very happy time for the earth. What we see here is part of the web of life. The tropical rain-forest is a co-operative effort – all the plants and animals seek a balance with everything else around. Through the passage of time conditions may change and creatures will change slightly, adapt. The urge to stay alive is uppermost.

"If you wonder why we call this place High Point and make a bit of a fuss here, it's because at this point in the long Journey of Wonders, humans begin to emerge."

"But where are they? I can't see any," I said.

"It's not a sudden arrival," replied Mother Gaia. "It'll take several million years, but the wonderful thing is that finally they will understand who they are and where they came from and how it all happened."

"You mean from the stars, from Tiamat, from the Very Beginning, don't you Mother Gaia," said Brydie.

"You've got it," she replied. "In this tropical forest there's everything they need to make a go of it."

"I think I get it too," I said. "Humans, all the people like Brydie and me will evolve from those strange looking chimps trying to stand up."

The Great Mother came back looking cool in a loosely draped long white dress and comfortable sandals. The Green Man gave each of us a garland of flowers to wear.

"We are ready for the ceremony, Mother Gaia. You may begin," said the Great Mother.

"Dear Brydie and Bran, as children of the universe and as earthlings representing the human race, we welcome you to this celebration. So let us affirm here together our place in the universe through the six directions.

"We look to the East, place of beginnings and of hope – and give our thanks.

"We look to the South, place of warmth and connectedness – and give our thanks.

"We look to the West, place of the heart and of intuition – and give our thanks.

"We look to the North, place of being and of wisdom – and give our thanks.

"We look down to the earth, place of life and human compassion – and give our thanks.

"We look up to the sky, place of clean air and freedom – and give our thanks."

First we all gathered in a loose group facing East and then moved around the circle of columns facing each direction. Mother Gaia spoke the words, "We look to..." and we answered with "and give our thanks."

Then we stood in the centre of the temple, looking towards the forest. The Green Man said: "I have made a new poem which I call 'I am here to Wonder'. I hope that you will like it.

> At the very beginning
> When All was a deep ocean of potential
> the Great Mother had a longing,
> a strong urge to reveal herself.
> So she called forth time, space, energy, matter and awareness
> and robed herself in cosmic splendour.
> I am here to wonder at the mystery of creation.
>
> I am here to wonder:
> at the universe newly come into being
> at the dance of hydrogen giving birth
> to millions of galaxies and stars over aeons of time.
> I am here to wonder at the beauty and vastness of the universe.
>
> I am here to wonder:
> at our own galaxy, the Milky Way,
> with our own sun and its planets,
> and at Gaia, planet of water
> birthing that first life in her warm shallow seas.
> I am here to wonder at the miracle of life.
>
> I am here to wonder:
> at the fantastic diversity of plants and animals,
> living and extinct,
> and at myself, member of the human species,
> all a unique expression of the divine creativity.
> I am here to wonder and give thanks.

"What a beautiful poem, Green Man," said the Great Mother. "We like it a lot."

Then we all sat down. Mother Gaia produced a tray with six large brown earthenware goblets of pure spring water. These were handed round and we all drank. The water was cool, sweet and surprisingly delicious.

"Without good, clean, free-flowing water life cannot flourish," said the Green Man.

Mother Gaia told us later that she had been given the goblets. They were made by a local potter in Burgundy. "There, people use them for drinking wine but I think they're just as suitable for water." Then she handed round a plate of small waffles. They were spicy and tasted of honey.

"Are these made of the best ingredients, Mother Gaia?" asked the Great Mother.

"Oh yes, I made them myself. They're all as nature intended."

"Good, may the bounty of the earth be available in equal measure to everyone."

I don't know exactly how it happened, but the conversation then turned on people's ages.

"There is no mystery about mine," volunteered Mother Gaia, "I am as old as the earth."

"And you Green Man?" we asked.

"Everyone knows that I'm as old as life itself. Let me see, that is about four thousand million years."

"Brydie and I are nearly the same age," I said. "Before all our time travelling started I was eleven and Brydie was ten.

We both looked at the Great Mother. She was smiling. She had welcomed us at the Very Beginning so she must be a lot older than that.

She guessed our thoughts and said, "I am forever."

There followed a long silence, nearly ten minutes, while we thought about all these things or listened to the noises of the forest. Brydie told me later that she felt very connected to everything, very comfortable and peaceful.

When we started talking again, I said that I had two questions. Firstly, I wasn't quite sure what the ceremony was all about, and secondly had someone not turned up?

"I'll answer the second question first," said the Green Man. "You saw correctly that there was a stool and a goblet and some biscuits too many. You see, there may be a late guest or a stranger. It means we're always ready.

"The first question is harder."

He then explained that humans keep on forgetting who they are. That they treat the earth as a resource for their own pleasures. They've forgotten that it's meant to be a sacred community of all living and non-living things. A ritual helps to connect body and soul and is a reminder that everything is a gift.

"Great Mother," said Brydie. "While we were silent, I felt so comfortable and peaceful and now I feel full of energy again."

"Would you sing one of your songs for us, Brydie?" she asked.

Brydie thought for a moment and than she sang:

> Trees grow tall in the heart of the forest
> High in the sky and their roots go down in the deep dark earth,

repeating this several times.

The Great Mother asked for another one, so she sang:

> In everything I see your beauty
> In everything I see your beauty
> In earth, in sky, in water, and in flames,
> I see the beauty of your love in everything,
> In everything.

"That was very lovely," said the Great Mother. We were all silent for a while. Then she left us to change back into her travel clothes.

Mother Gaia left as well to do some tidying up and while I talked to the Green Man, Brydie slipped away and joined the chimps just for a little while. We had seen a film called *Gorillas in the Mist* about a young woman called Dian Fossey who lived with them. She would have stayed longer but Mother Gaia called out in a rather stern voice, "Brydie, come back at once. We've been looking everywhere for you."

Brydie explained that she just longed to be with them. There was a mother feeding her baby, and the mother didn't seem to mind her being there.

"We understand," said the Great Mother.

Mother Gaia was called away on urgent business but she promised to catch up with us later. There was no time to lose. The Great Mother slung her bag over her shoulder and took us by the hand. We were off again. The Green Man followed behind. What adventure was waiting for us next on our Journey of Wonders? It struck me that there was not much of the journey left in which to find the Triple Mirror.

14

The Circle of Masks

Our last adventure turned out to be even more exciting than the previous ones. Mother Gaia was detained elsewhere (what exactly was she doing 'elsewhere' we wondered) so the Green Man was asked to take her place again. In some ways the scene around us looked familiar.

"I think we're in America and this is surely Indian country," I exclaimed with delight.

"Well guessed Bran," said the Green Man. "But remember, this is not the Present, this is North America ten thousand years ago.

"And you, Brydie, what do you see?"

"I see two groups of tepees – some distance from one another along a stream. Beyond on the left there's a wood with quite a lot of birch trees," she replied, "and I see red skinned people."

At last we were seeing humans like ourselves.

"It's taken them an extremely long time from the Very Beginning!" I said.

"Well said, Bran," said the Green Man. "I find them handsome and relaxed and they look as if they truly belong here."

"I see mountains in the distance," interrupted Brydie.

"Yes, the descendants of these people here will call them the Bighorn Mountains. They're over four thousand metres high. They're named after the sheep that live there. The water of the river over there will eventually flow into the mighty Missouri and then into the Mississippi to finish its journey in the Atlantic Ocean.

"What else do you see? There's something important that you haven't seen before on your journey."

We looked around and thought really hard. "We give up," I said.

"Speak for yourself," said Brydie, but she soon gave up too. "You'll have to tell us."

"Grass," said the Green Man.

"Is that all!" I replied, "Is that so important?"

"Definitely," said the Green Man. "You see, most plants grow at the top, and if this gets eaten the plant dies or has to start over again from its roots. Grass is different, the leaves of grass grow from the bottom and if Amber here eats the top of a leaf it simply keeps on growing, so she can come back later and eat some more.

"Big grasslands like the ones you can see here can provide food for lots of animals, big ones like buffalo as well as small ones like Amber. Without the buffalo the people here would not survive."

This gave us lots to think about. We were silent for a while just looking around. Dogs were lying in the sunshine or walking about with their noses into things. Children were helping their parents with the chores. A boy of my age was helping his father to build a canoe; I wished it were me. These people of 10,000 years ago didn't seem in any hurry. They took their time over everything.

But all of a sudden the pace quickened. It looked as if they were getting ready for something. Some drumming started up and people began to gather on a particularly flat bit of ground where they sat down in a big circle.

"What's going to happen?" we both asked the Green Man, when some chanting started.

"There's going to be a Council meeting," he replied. "Let me put you in the picture. These people come here every summer, and so did their ancestors, to hunt the buffalo. Their chants tell them of the brave deeds of their ancestors – how they killed the buffalo and survived. You see, it provides them with excellent meat, hides, sinews and bones for making tools. But with only stone and bone tools and weapons it is quite difficult to kill a buffalo. It is dangerous as well: it's a fierce animal.

"Our two groups of native Americans here have recently had success in the hunt. But there is a serious problem. The upstream group has dumped two carcasses in the river hoping that the water would clean the bones, and a woman from the downstream group is now claiming that her five year old boy is ill from drinking water from downriver. Are you following me?" We both nodded.

Next, we watched a wood fire being lit in the centre of the circle. I counted about thirty people in the circle. I spotted two people who looked like Elders; and there was a woman with a sick looking boy sitting next to them. The circle wasn't complete and I wondered who else was expected. The chanting and drumming went on and on. Then suddenly there was a hush. Quite a few people were putting on face-masks. This was followed by a dead silence. The only noise was the wind in the birch trees. Then one of the Elders stood up and spoke with a clear voice. Not until later did we realise that he was saying a prayer invoking the Great Spirit to open the Council. Then a brief pause.

The Great Mother who had been silent since we arrived asked us if we would like to put on masks too and join in. "I can arrange it. Choose an animal or plant," she said. "You'll soon get the hang of things, I promise."

"Oh yes please, Great Mother," we both said in chorus. "I'd like to be a snake – a water snake," I said, thinking of Nessie and Scotland.

"I'd like to be a tree," said Brydie, "a willow or perhaps a birch." The Great Mother always seemed to have just the right things in her bag.

"Go and sit where you can see a gap in the circle," said the Green Man. "That is what it's for. To let something new join in the Council."

So that was it. Something new. We were accepted by the group without a fuss. As soon as we were seated the Elder told the assembled company why he had called both groups together. Then he picked up a stick decorated with feathers, beadwork and little bones and passed it to the person on his left. We soon got the hang of what was going on. In fact I had read about such meetings in one of my adventure books. And here were Brydie and I actually taking part! It was magic. The most amazing thing was that we could understand their language without difficulty, another of the Great Mother's gifts, no doubt. Everyone was allowed to speak 'from the heart' while he or she was holding the talking stick. All the others were then listening 'with the heart'. If you didn't want to speak you just passed the talking stick to your neighbour. People with facemasks spoke for that particular animal. Children are encouraged to choose an animal or plant quite young. They learn all they can about its habits and find out what the animal or plant is teaching them. In that way they can speak for them in a Council when they grow up.

We listened to quite a few speakers. The sun was sinking fast in the west. The fire was well alight and a welcome source of warmth on this late summer's day.

Someone spoke for Mountain: "In winter I'm covered by clean white snow that falls from the sky. My meltwaters form beautiful brooks to become streams and rivers. Everywhere creatures come to drink my pure water. Let's keep it that way."

Mayfly spoke for the insects who spend most of their lifecycle in water: "We like fast flowing water and hide under rocks where we catch tiny creatures. If the water is polluted they become sick and so do we. We may die, then there is no food for fishes."

Trout spoke: "If I eat bad food my body gets sick. I wither away. My body can no longer feed the red man, the red woman and the children."

When it came to my turn, I was still wondering what to say when I was handed the talking stick. This is what I said while my heart was beating fast: "I'm a water snake. I like to slither in damp grass and swim in nice cool pools. I could easily swim to another part of the river if I sensed that the water was fouling. But I prefer to stay here. You see, I know this patch. This is where I belong. So let us keep the river clean."

Then it was Brydie's turn. I handed her the stick. "Trees need water every day," she said. "We draw it up from the ground with our many roots and it passes to our leaves. Our willow branches are very pliable and we give them to the red man and his woman. The bark makes good medicine. We like our roots very damp and prefer nice clean water for our health. When I am birch tree, my buds unfurl early in the year and are a welcome sign of spring for all the creatures. My bark when I am fully grown makes good material for canoes. The wind loves to play in my branches. It is music which we give to all the creatures. So you see, trees too need good water."

"Brydie that was a long speech – so beautiful," I whispered, I took her hand and squeezed it.

It would be too long to give a full account of all that went on. The other Elder spoke and it became clear that the upstream people had agreed to remove the carcasses from the water and to dispose of them in their customary way. The Elder who had opened the Council with prayer made a final speech.

He said that the rivers were our brothers. That they quench the thirst of all living things. He reminded us that all things live in co-operation and that we had an obligation to honour the rivers. "The land is sacred," he said. "We would die of a great loneliness of spirit if ever we forgot this truth."

15

The Triple Mirror

$\mathcal{T}$he fire glowed in the dark. It was very still for a moment. We were completely engrossed in what had been happening. The two Elders looked at each other and nodded as if in silent agreement about something. One of them picked up a large buffalo hide bag and carrying it carefully between them they walked slowly towards us. The boy who had been building the canoe joined them, carrying a large rug. It seemed right that we should stand up to meet them. The boy spread out the colourful, patterned rug. The Elders gestured that we should sit down on it. Then the bag was opened and the Elders carefully lifted something out of it which looked like a large book. Holding it so that we could see, one of the Elders opened it – it was the Triple Mirror!

At last! It shone with a magic brightness as if light came from within. We were speechless. It was dazzlingly beautiful.

The Elders gestured, inviting us to take a closer look.

"Mother Gaia said the Mirror was specially for you, Brydie," I said. "Why don't you look first?"

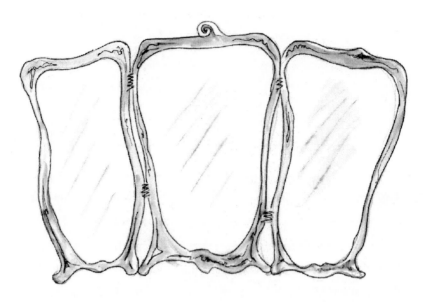

"It's big enough for both of us to look at the same time," she replied.

We looked first of all into the mirror on the left. We saw the fire and the circle but that soon vanished. We saw scenes that we soon realised were part of our marvellous journey, but time was running backwards. It was weird. We saw dinosaurs roaming over vast plains, which quickly disappeared under the sea. We saw the continents moving southwards until they gathered over the South Pole. We saw the early earth bombarded by comets and asteroids. Then the earth itself dissolved into fragments. The vast cloud that was Tiamat shrank and coalesced into a star. Then came the long unbuilding of the galaxies. And finally we saw the face of the Great Mother looming out of the clouds of Hydrogen. The whole beautiful story unwound before our eyes in just a few minutes.

Then we looked at the middle mirror. All we could see was our own reflections, as if this was just an ordinary mirror. "What does this mean?" I asked, wondering whether I would get a reply from anybody. I didn't.

So we looked into the right hand mirror. What we saw was very confusing. It started with the dead jungle where our journey had started, and there was Akka, the she-wolf, looking straight at us. Then there was a confusing succession of pictures. Clearly this was the future. Prospering forests and lakes mixed in with scenes of desolation, both desert and arctic cold. Happy people living in elegant towns were blown away by floods and storms. Although it was frightening we felt we had to go on looking. But there was no clear ending; the mirror slowly went blank and we could see nothing more.

We looked at each other but could find nothing to say. It was all too much for words. The two Elders who had been patiently holding the Triple Mirror seemed to understand. They simply put it back into its bag and slowly walked back to their places in the circle. They asked everybody to stand and they then said together, "All our Relations."

The whole circle replied with, "All our Relations."

I wasn't quite sure what this meant but I guessed it included Akka the wolf and her friends. "Find the Triple Mirror" she had said. Well, the mirror had found us and we'd looked into it, but was that enough?

"Don't we need to take the Mirror with us?" whispered Brydie.

"Let's ask the Great Mother," I replied.

Then there was a stirring and people took off their face masks and started talking. Large bowls of hot berry juice were handed round followed by a tasty bannock. The refreshment was very welcome. Some chanting started up again. It seemed the right moment for us to slip away. We made a farewell gesture to the Elders, rejoined the Great Mother and returned our masks.

"Great Mother," said Brydie, "we need your help with what we saw in the Triple Mirror."

"Could we ask for it so we can take it home with us?" I added. "I'm sure they'd give it to you, if you asked for it."

She smiled, "I'm sure they would. But it is in good hands here. They are good people who think about the future more than most. I think it should stay with them. You are not the only ones who have looked in the Triple Mirror and others will come who will also see what you have seen. You see, in a sense you are the Triple Mirror, you don't need to take it with you.

"You need no help from me, Brydie. You have learnt enough to make sense of what you saw. That's why you have made the journey.

"I will say this. What you saw of the future, both the good and the bad, may or may not happen. It's not fixed or certain. Be guided by the past; be aware of the possibilities of the future but live and act in the present."

"Of course! That's what the centre mirror was telling us, wasn't it?" Said Brydie.

"You see," said the Great Mother. "You don't need my help, do you?"

"But what did they mean by 'All our Relations'?" I asked. "Does it mean all the animals and plants as well as people?"

"Yes, Bran" she replied, "But also the rivers and the mountains and the wind and the sun and the moon."

The Green Man joined us. "I really like the way they do things here," he said.

"You mean consulting all living beings?" asked Brydie, "a kind of Council of all Beings."

"Yes Brydie" he replied.

"Why not a United Nations Council of all Beings, UNCAB for short?" I suggested.

"Just a minute, Bran," said the Green Man. "Don't you know about 'small is beautiful'? We must make it work first at the local level, like our friends here."

"Yes, but…" I would have gone on, but Mother Gaia suddenly reappeared.

"I have grave news. There has been a big earthquake in Indonesia. Planet Earth always keeps me fully occupied. I won't be able to stay long, Great Mother."

"While you were away Brydie and Bran have been shown the Triple Mirror," said the Great Mother.

Mother Gaia looked hard at both of us. "Yes, I can see that they have, that's good – our journey is nearly over then."

"Mother Gaia is right" she went on. "Your journey is nearly over. It is time to return you to the Present."

I was very happy to be going home but disappointed that, after all the travelling, we couldn't take the Triple Mirror with us. I still had some questions about Akka the wolf and how, finding the Mirror was about finding ourselves. I looked at Brydie – we had a lot of talking to do when we got home.

So all of us, the Great Mother, Mother Gaia, the Green Man, Brydie holding Amber and I with Corax on my shoulder, got ready to finish our journey. For the last time our boots would do the travelling.

16

Farewell

$\mathcal{I}$n no time at all we reached the edge of the Present. The long and incredible Journey of Wonders was coming to an end. We were back in the Great Glen with Loch Ness slowly emerging out of the clearing mist. We were back where we had started our amazing adventure and we seemed to have been away for no time at all.

"I am returning you to the safety of the Present," said the Great Mother, "for that is where you and Brydie and Corax and Amber live and where you belong."

There was no look and learn. We took off our suits, yellow boots and goggles and gave them to the Great Mother. It was time to say goodbye.

Mother Gaia and the Green Man gave us a big hug. The Green Man made a bit of a fuss over the animals saying: "Goodbye little fellows – so pleased to have met you." Then Mother Gaia and the Green Man started to fade away, waving with both hands until we could see them no more.

Now we were alone with the Great Mother, as we had been at the Very Beginning.

"Great Mother," I said. "You have shown us the past and it was often frightening and wonderful at the same time. And we have seen some of the possibilities for the future in the Triple Mirror and it's also going to be both frightening and wonderful."

She took both my hands in hers and answered, "Dear Bran, I have shown you where you have come from. From the Very Beginning, through the births and deaths of galaxies and stars and of countless creatures. We have journeyed together through the story of the universe up to the Present. The journey goes on, but where it will lead I do not know. It cannot be known until it is given birth and that is your task, Bran and Brydie. You now know where you have come from and that will help you to find out where you are going."

"It is so lovely to know that we will always be in your story, Great Mother," said Brydie, "and that we can help you make it come true."

"Dear Brydie, I love you and Bran very much," she said taking Brydie's hands in hers.

Then she opened her bag and took out two beautiful apples. She handed one to each of us, saying: "Farewell, dear star children – always be generous."

And before we had time to say thank you for an absolutely wonderful time she had gone and so had the mist. It was suddenly very still. The loch and the mountains looked so clear we felt we could just reach out and touch them. We must have stayed there in a happy daze for some time, because the next thing we knew was that it was late afternoon. We still had the apples in our hands but Corax and Amber had vanished. We just had time to make it back to the cottage for Mrs McPherson's Halloween celebration.

Mum and Dad were really glad to see us.

"Where have you been all this time?" asked Mum anxiously.

How could we answer?

Brydie went straight for the peat fire to get warm.

"Look Bran. Over the fireplace, there's a mirror here too."

"What are you two on about?" asked Dad.

Before we could reply there was a knock on the door. It was Mrs MacPherson with some griddle cakes and scones.

"I see you've got some apples," she said. And she gave us a look as if she already knew that we had them. "I told you that at Halloween the veil between the present and the past is thin."

"All we need now is some butter and jam to have a real Halloween tea. Everything else can wait."

We looked thankfully at Mrs MacPherson as we sat down and tackled her griddlecakes. They were delicious — it was good to be home.

"Thank you Mother Gaia," we whispered. "Thank you, Great Mother."

About the Authors

Erna Chrispeels inherited a passion for nature from her father who was a keen gardener. She feels called to use her training as a biologist to awaken people to the irreparable damage we are inflicting on the Earth.. In 1999 she published a collection of poems, *A Spark in My Soul, Awakening Spirituality in an Ecological Age.*

Michael Colebrook's fascination with the natural world was stimulated by long hours spent gazing into a small stream that ran across the bottom of the family garden. After training in zoology, his interest moved firstly to Windermere and then to the North Atlantic Ocean in a career of research on the ecology of marine plankton. He is the author of many scientific papers and has also produced a GreenSpirit pamphlet *The New Universe Story.*

Together they edited *Earthsong, a Green Anthology* of *Poetry, Readings and Prayers* in 1990 and co-authored a GreenSpirit pamphlet *Walking the Sacred Story* in 2000.

Meier Williams studied at Wimbledon School of Art and at Croydon College where she gained her HND in theatre design. She has used the arts to work in the community for the last thirteen years. She lives in Cornwall and is happily married with two children. In her spare time she enjoys working in the world of the theatre as a costume and set designer.